MATHNET™ CASEBOOK

#4 The Map With a Gap

By David D. Connell and Jim Thurman

Illustrated by Danny O'Leary

Scientific
BOOKS FOR YOUNG READERS
American

Children's Television Workshop
W. H. Freeman/New York

Scientific American Books for Young Readers
is an imprint of W.H. Freeman and Company,
41 Madison Avenue, New York, New York 10010

On **MATHNET**, the role of George Frankly is played
by Joe Howard; the role of Kate Monday is
played by Beverly Leech; the role of Chief Thad Green
is played by James Earl Jones; and the role of
Bronco Guillermo Gomez is played by Ben Hoag.

Cover photo of Joe Howard, Beverly Leech, and Ben Hoag ©
CTW/Richard Termine

Illustrated by Danny O'Leary

Activities by Richard Chevat

Activity illustrations by Lynn Brunelle

Library of Congress Cataloging-in-Publication Data

Connell, David D.

The map with a gap: Mathnet Casebook/by David D. Connell and Jim Thurman.

p. cm.

Summary: Mathnet detectives Kate Monday and George Frankly use math skills like triangulation and scale to find a buried treasure in a ghost town.

ISBN 0-7167-6527-6 (hard).—ISBN 0-7167-6523-3 (soft)

[1. Mystery and detective stories. 2. Buried treasure—Fiction.]

PZ7.C761853Map 1994

[Fic]—dc20   93-37779

                                                                    CIP

                                                                    AC

Printed in the United States of America

10 9 8 7 6 5 4 3 2 1

CHAPTER

1

"George," said Kate Monday, covering the mouthpiece of the telephone she was holding. "Do we have an appointment with a *cowboy*?"

"I don't think so, Kate." George Frankly looked as puzzled as the crossword he had been working. Then a smile spread across his face. "But I *hope* so. I love cowboys. I wanted to be one when I was a kid, but then it turned out I was allergic to cows, so I had to find another line of work."

"That's very interesting, George," Kate said impatiently, "but there's a cowboy waiting to see us."

George checked his desk calendar and said, "There are no cowboys scheduled, but what the heck."

"Send him in, please," Kate said into the phone.

Over the years the two detectives from Mathnet had played host to a number of unusual citizens. There had been a hot air balloonist, a masked wrestler, a joke-telling parrot, and even a scientist who claimed he could control the weather . . . but never an honest-to-gosh *cowboy*. They turned toward the door in anticipation.

"Maybe it'll be a movie cowboy," George said enthusiastically, smoothing his hair, "like Roy Rogers or Clint Eastwood."

"Don't get your hopes up, Pard," Kate said. But she, too, stared at the door in excited anticipation.

The door opened, and a cowboy walked in.

"You're not Clint Eastwood," said George, trying to hide his disappointment.

The cowboy standing in the office was a ten-year-old boy wearing chaps, a Western shirt, and a vest. His ten-gallon hat rested on the ears of his five-gallon head.

"I'm Bronco Guillermo Gomez," said the handsome youth. He thrust out his hand to Kate, who shook it and offered him a chair.

"Sit down, Bronco," she said with a smile. "I'm Kate Monday."

"Sure, Bronco, take a load off your spurs," said George, recovering from his surprise. "I'm George Frankly."

"Thanks," said Bronco. He put his backpack on the floor and sat down.

"What can we do for you, Bronco?" Kate asked, reseating herself and smiling at their visitor.

"Well, Ms. Monday . . . I need you to help me find something," Bronco began.

Kate made a note in her casebook. "Something you lost?" she prompted Bronco.

"No." Bronco shook his head. "I didn't lose it."

"Who did?" George asked. Without waiting for an answer he continued, "Was it your little sister? Probably it was his little sister," George said to Kate knowingly. "My little sister used to lose my stuff all the time."

Kate looked at her partner and rolled her eyes.

Bronco shook his head so hard his hat slipped down over his nose. "No, no. Saddlesore Capone lost it," Bronco said, pushing his hat back up, away from his eyes.

"If Saddlesore Capone lost it, why not ask him to help find it?" Kate reasoned.

"Because Saddlesore didn't really *lose* it," Bronco explained. "He sort of *hid* it."

Kate shook her head. Bronco had been in the office for under two minutes, and already this case was confusing. "Maybe you'd better start at the beginning, Bronco," she suggested.

"Well . . . " Bronco cleared his throat. "At the beginning Saddlesore Capone robbed a stagecoach."

"I didn't see anything about that in the newspapers," George said. "But I mostly just look at the crosswords."

"He did it in 1853, Mr. Frankly," Bronco explained. "Saddlesore robbed the stage of its gold and hid it. No one has seen it since."

"How much gold did he get?" Kate asked, her eyebrows raised. This was the first stagecoach robbery Mathnet had been asked to investigate.

"Lots," Bronco said excitedly. "Fifteen pounds. It

was worth about $3,600 back in 1853."

"The gold would be worth a lot more today. Gold is about $500 an ounce now," George said. He did some quick figuring. "Fifteen pounds . . . 16 ounces to the pound is . . ."

Bronco started shaking his head again. After he'd pushed his hat back up he corrected George. "Not *16* ounces, Mr. Frankly. When you're measuring gold you use the troy system."

"The troy system is English," Kate said, "and it has 12 ounces to the pound. Saddlesore stole 15 pounds." She smiled at George. "I'll race you, Pard."

George picked up pencil and paper while Kate grabbed a calculator and began punching numbers.

"So 12 times 15 is 180." Kate was thinking aloud. "One hundred eighty ounces at $500 per ounce . . ."

Kate stared at her calculator and let out a low whistle just as George announced loudly, "$90,000!"

Bronco nodded happily.

George was impressed. "Gee, that's almost enough to have dinner in Beverly Hills."

"And no one has ever found it?" Kate asked.

"Not until now." Bronco smiled from ear to ear. "But now *I* know where it is."

"You do?" George and Kate stared at the young buckaroo in disbelief.

"Well . . ." Bronco's smile faded. "Sort of." When he saw Kate and George's disappointed expressions, he started digging wildly through his backpack. "But I do have this!"

He pulled a sheet of paper out of his backpack

and spread it on the desk. The corners were ragged, and the folds were beginning to tear. Bronco had obviously been carrying the paper around in his crowded bag for some time.

George and Kate leaned over for a look.

"What's this? A map?" George asked, perking up again.

"Yes, sir." Bronco nodded enthusiastically. His hat threatened to slide all the way down again, but he shoved it back up just in time.

"See, I go camping around there a lot with my folks," Bronco explained. "I heard a story about the missing gold a couple of years ago and got curious. This is a tracing of the map found on Saddlesore when he died. I found it in a library and copied it," he said proudly.

Kate bent forward to study the map. "And you think this is a map showing where he hid the treasure?"

"Uh huh." Bronco nodded.

George looked at the map more closely and said, "It doesn't look like a treasure map, Bronco."

Kate stared at her partner in surprise. "How can you tell?" she asked.

"There's no X to mark the spot," George pointed out. "Don't treasure maps always have an X to mark the spot where the loot is buried?"

"That's what everybody thought," Bronco said.

"Everybody?" Kate's eyebrows shot up. "You mean *lots* of people know about this treasure?"

"Sure. People have known about the treasure for

almost 150 years and they've known of the map for nearly that long, too. But no one ever found the X." Bronco shrugged. "So they gave up."

"What makes you think *you've* found something, Bronco?" Kate asked, smiling warmly. Bronco was obviously dying for them to ask. He was practically bursting the buttons of his Western shirt with pride.

"This," said Bronco dramatically. He whipped a shiny aluminum thermos bottle from his bag and waved it under George's nose. "See what happens when you look closely at it," he said.

George took the metal bottle and stared at his reflection. "I see that I need a haircut," he said, smoothing back his hair.

Bronco sighed in exasperation and took back the thermos. "It reflects, right?" he asked eagerly.

"Right," agreed George.

"So?" Kate added.

"So watch what happens when I put the bottle right here on the map." Bronco's tongue stuck out at one corner of his mouth as he carefully positioned the bottle on the map. He gave it a final tap to move it to the left and then pointed triumphantly at the bottle.

Kate and George leaned toward it and stared. Squiggles on the map that had appeared to be contour lines indicating elevations suddenly took on a new meaning in the warped reflection of the rounded bottle.

"I can see something that looks like a rock," Kate said excitedly. "And a tree. And some of the lines form letters when they're reflected in the thermos," she

added, peering closer.

"I'll be doggoned," George said, slipping into cowboy talk in his excitement. He pointed to the map. "It
says 'Dig heer.'"

Bronco grinned with delight. "Saddlesore Capone
wasn't much of a speller, so I figure that means 'Dig
here.'" Bronco stabbed his finger at that spot on the
map. "This must be where he hid the treasure."

"That's amazing, Bronco." Kate stared at the cowboy in admiration.

"Uh huh." Bronco nodded. His hat began inching down again. "Saddlesore Capone used a cylindrical mirror to hide his message and I just stumbled on it."

"Incredible," George agreed. "You say people have been looking for the treasure since . . . ?"

"Since 1853," Bronco answered.

"And after all these years, Bronco Guillermo Gomez has figured it out. Congratulations, Bronco," George congratulated Bronco.

"Thanks, Mr. Frankly." Bronco smiled and blushed. His hat slid over his face, and he paused a moment before pushing it back up. When he did his smile was gone again. "There's still one little problem. And that's why I need your help."

George and Kate looked quizzically at the short cowboy.

Bronco shrugged. "I don't know where to dig."

George pointed to the map. "You dig here," he said, thumping the words "Dig heer" with his index finger.

"But," Bronco asked, "*where* is 'here' ?"

Kate and George looked at the map and then at each other. They had a map all right, but a map of what? Bronco was right. They didn't know where "here" was. The gold was still lost.

DUM DE DUM DUM

CHAPTER
2

"I see what you mean," said Chief Thad Green. "This map was drawn many years ago. The landmarks drawn on it may have changed. That rock and tree might not even be there anymore."

It was a few minutes later. Kate and George were in the Chief's office and had just explained the problem to their Mathnet boss.

"Yes, sir," Kate said, "and the only way we can try to orient the map is to go to the last place Saddlesore was spotted and see if we can get a fix."

"Where was that?" the Chief asked, leaning back in his office chair. The chair protested with a loud creak.

"It was in a town called Mulch Gulch, in the high desert about 100 miles northeast of here," Bronco answered. He had joined the detectives in their meeting with the chief. "It's a ghost town now, Chief Green."

"*Ghost* town?" George echoed.

"You're not afraid of ghosts, are you, George?" Chief Green teased.

"No, of course not," George answered, "because there are no such things as ghosts. But even so . . . a whole *town* full of them?"

"Don't worry, Mr. Frankly. No one lives there anymore," Bronco said. "Not even ghosts." He frowned. "At least, I don't think so."

"Mulch Gulch, huh?" Chief Green rubbed his chin thoughtfully. "I've never heard of it."

"Mulch Gulch was a thriving mining town for years," Bronco said, proud to show off the history he'd been studying in his search for the gold.

"What happened?" Kate wanted to know.

"In the early 1880s the vein of gold the prospectors had found just petered out," Bronco said. "With no gold, there wasn't any other reason to stay, so people abandoned the town," he added with a shrug.

"Hmmmm." Chief Green stared thoughtfully at the map. Kate and Bronco looked eagerly at the Mathnet boss. George just looked nervous.

"Well, things around Mathnet HQ are rather quiet," the Chief said. "I think you should accompany young Bronco to Mulch Gulch and see what you can find."

"Thanks, Chief Green," Kate said. "We're on our way."

"Yeah, thanks, Chief Green," George echoed. But he didn't sound happy.

* * *

Before heading for the desert, the Mathnetters made a few stops. George and Kate stopped at their homes to pick up clothes and supplies. Then they drove to Bronco's house. They wanted to get his parents' permission to take the treasure-seeker to Mulch Gulch.

"By all means," Bronco's father said. "But I warn you, Mathnetters . . .Guillermo is *fanático* about this treasure business. You may be biting off more than you can chew."

"*Aquí*," said Bronco's mother, holding up a small basket. "I've packed some food for you." She handed the basket to George.

George peered inside the basket at a stack of round, thin cornmeal cakes. "What are these? Edible Frisbees?"

Mr. and Mrs. Gomez burst into laughter. "Those are tortillas," said Mrs. Gomez.

"They're homemade and delicious," her husband added. He gave George a healthy slap on the back as he laughed loudly. "*Loco gringo*," he managed to say between chuckles.

Bronco loaded his gear in the back of George's old station wagon. Then he tried to climb inside, but his mother wrapped him in a hug and kissed his cheek. "*Cuidarse*," she said.

"I'll take care," Bronco promised, wiggling out of the hug and wiping his cheek. He ducked into the backseat before his mother could hug him again.

"All aboard for Mulch Gulch," announced George, as his vehicle coughed and sputtered and lurched its way toward the highway.

"*Ay, que loco*," Mr. Gomez chuckled.

* * *

Kate, George, and Bronco had traveled the interstate for nearly two hours when the threesome heard the whine of a distant siren. It quickly grew louder.

"Oh, brother . . . am I speeding?" George pounded his fist on the battered steering wheel. "Not another ticket," he moaned.

Kate surveyed the rusty bucket of bolts in which she was riding. The seats were losing their stuffing, and the dashboard looked like it was missing a few instruments. "The only way this old heap could break a speed limit would be if you drove it off a cliff," she said.

"Maybe they'll give us a ticket for slowing," Bronco suggested, watching the scenery crawl past. He turned to look through the rear window. "Hey, Mr. Frankly . . ."

"What?"

"That's no police car." Bronco said hesitantly as he squinted. "That's an *ec-nal-ub-ma*." Bronco managed to sound out the word he couldn't read. "The letters are all backwards."

"A what?" George asked, as he looked in his dusty rearview mirror. Smiling, he said, "I'll just pull over and let it pass." George lifted his foot from the gas pedal and steered the station wagon to the shoulder of the road.

A siren-spouting vehicle shot by in a blur of red and white.

"That ec-nal-ub-ma looks a lot like an ambulance to me," Kate said.

"I get it. They write the word backward and reverse the letters," Bronco said. "That way, when drivers look in their rearview mirrors, the word makes sense."

"Right, Bronco. You're one smart *hombre*," George said. He pressed the gas again and the car lurched back onto the road.

The day, which had begun warm and sunny, turned cloudy and gray as they drove deeper into the desert. The wind howled through the loose doors and windows of George's old car. George looked nervously out at the empty desert, waiting for the first glimpse of the ghost town.

Suddenly, Bronco cried, "Wait! Stop!"

George hit the brakes, and the car stuttered to a stop. The engine spluttered and died.

"What? What?" George asked, looking around wildly for a possible ghost.

"Sorry," Bronco apologized. "I didn't mean to scare you. It's just that we're about to pass the library where I found the stuff on Saddlesore." He pointed to a building perched on a red rock bluff above them.

"A library?" George wiped his brow. "Is that all?"

"I just thought you might like to check the tracing I made of Saddlesore's map," Bronco said in a small voice.

"Couldn't hurt," Kate said, smiling at Bronco. She

glanced at her partner. "Relax, George!"

George forced a smile and started the car. He drove toward the Kern County Library.

Late afternoon clouds gathered as the car pulled to a stop. The threesome climbed from the car and started up the library steps.

"I don't like the looks of this weather," George said, looking at the sky. Distant thunder rumbled to the north, signaling a possible storm.

Bronco opened the library's massive oak door and they entered. The library was dark. Dark and empty. Bronco pointed to a desk where George and Kate saw a thin, cadaverous-looking man. His pale face, framed by slicked-back black hair, glowed eerily in the dim light. Perched on his nose was a pair of spectacles. On the desk in front of him was a sign that read D. John Mutard, Librarian.

George approached the desk. The man was totally engrossed, examining some 3-by-5 cards. George stared, admiring the man's sleek black three-piece suit and his string tie. The librarian didn't look up.

"Excuse me," George said.

D. John Mutard jumped out of his chair in surprise. Then he put a bony finger to his lips. "Shhhhh!!!" he whispered fiercely. "Puh-lease have some respect for the others."

George and Kate looked around. There were no others in the library. They looked at each other with raised eyebrows, but decided to play along with Mr. D. John Mutard.

"Sorry," George whispered respectfully. "I was wondering if we might see the archives of Mulch Gulch."

Mutard looked suspiciously at George and then at Kate. Then he looked down and spotted Bronco. His frown smoothed away. "Oh, hello, Bronco," he said in a friendlier whisper. "I didn't see you."

"These are friends of mine, Mr. Mutard," Bronco explained.

"We're detectives," Kate said in a low library voice. "I'm Kate Monday and this is my partner . . . "

" . . . George," George began in his normal voice then noticed Mutard's frown and finished in a whisper. " . . . Frankly. Mathnet."

"Mathnet?" Mutard lips thinned. Then he smiled. "Still looking for that treasure, Bronco?" he asked.

Bronco blushed and nodded.

The librarian smiled condescendingly. "Bronco has been poring over the history of Mulch Gulch for months," he told Kate and George. "I keep telling him that hidden gold story is a myth."

Bronco frowned and inched away toward the history section.

"Thousands have searched for the gold without a trace," Mutard continued. "But Bronco insists it's there. I like his spirit, but it's a hopeless task, I fear."

Out of earshot, Bronco had pulled down a large tome. He put it on a table, and motioned to Kate and George. They left Mutard at his desk and strolled over for a look at Bronco's book.

"Here's the map I traced," Bronco said, pointing down at the opened book. George placed the tracing over the map in the book. They matched perfectly.

"Perfect," George exclaimed, his voice booming in the empty room.

"Shhhhh!!!" Mutard chastised them, pursing his thin lips.

"Sorry," George whispered, looking about. "I forgot about the others."

Mutard came over to see what the excitement was about. "Well, Bronco," he said, examining the map tracing, "maybe you *are* onto something this time. I wish you good luck in your quest."

"Thanks, Mr. Mutard," Bronco muttered. "We'll need to borrow some of these history books," he added, pulling some more books from the shelves.

"Thanks for your help," Kate said, shaking hands with the meek-mannered bibliophile. "Any advice before we hit the desert?"

"Well, let's see . . . ." Mutard counted off on his long, thin fingers. "Take plenty of blankets; it gets cold at night. Be sure you ride sturdy, surefooted horses . . . ."

"Horses?" George interrupted.

Kate looked sternly at Bronco. "Horses?"

Bronco stared at the floor. "I guess I forgot to tell you," he muttered. "The only way to get to Mulch Gulch from here is on horseback."

"Wait a minute," George said. His voice started to exit the whisper stage. "Horses don't like me. They resent my sitting on top of them. I don't know how to *drive* them." George's voice was heading straight for the shout category.

"If you can drive that car, you can 'drive' a horse." Kate said in her best supportive voice. She patted her

partner on the shoulder, then pushed him gently toward the door. "You'll love it, George. Now, let's go, buckaroos."

Mutard slid in front of Kate, blocking the door. He raised one white finger in warning. "One last thing of which to beware," he cautioned in an ominous whisper.

"Does it have anything to do with desperadoes?" George asked hopefully. He poked out his hands to mimic guns. "'We don't need no stinkin' badges,'" he growled.

"George, we do have badges," Kate said, puzzled.

"It's from a movie, Kate," George explained. "A *cowboy* movie."

"With desperadoes," Bronco added.

The three treasure-seekers headed out the door.

Mutard harrumphed to get their attention. The three of them looked back at the bony librarian framed in the shadowy doorway. "There aren't any desperadoes out there." Mutard sniffed.

"I'm glad to hear that," said Kate. George looked a little disappointed.

"But there *is* one man you should watch out for," Mutard continued, "a foxy old desert rat named Rommel. Scruffy Rommel."

The door began to swing closed.

"What about this Rommel?" Kate asked.

"Just be careful of him, that's all." The librarian's spooky whisper came through the half-closed door. "Be *real* careful."

Thunder rumbled in the distance. The door slammed shut.

DUM DE DUM DUM

CHAPTER
3

Back in the car, Bronco pointed the way to Hobson's Stables. He told his new friends that Hobson's was where they would rent their mounts for the next leg of the journey. The stables were housed in a ramshackle barn under the proprietorship of a ramshackle blacksmith named Tobias Hobson.

"You're in luck," Tobias said. "I've got three animals left. I'll saddle 'em up for you."

"Thanks, Mr. Hobson," Bronco said.

"Let's get into our gear," Kate suggested to George.

The two detectives slipped into some empty stalls and changed from their Mathnet uniforms into more suitable Western garb. Kate emerged wearing boots, jeans, a denim shirt, a vest, and a cowboy hat. George looked like a dude without a ranch. He wore a satin shirt with fringe on the sleeves, a damask vest, hand-tooled leather boots, a large white hat, and a heavy leather gun belt with a holster strapped to his leg.

"How do I look?" George asked, walking out with a rolling gait. He stumbled as his spurs snagged on the splintery floor.

"Ya look like the guy John Wayne always beats up on in them moving picture shows," said Tobias Hobson. After tossing saddles up onto two horses, he paused to give George a long look. "You *do* know there's no six-shooter in your holster," he said.

"Don't believe in guns, stranger," George drawled, getting into his new role. Suddenly, he spun on his boot heels. "Go for leather!" he said, pulling a hand calculator from his holster. George spun the instrument around his finger, tossed it in the air, and dropped it deftly back into the holster.

"Very impressive," Kate said, nodding her head approvingly. "I'll feel safe if we're attacked by outlaw accountants."

"You're all set, folks," Tobias said. He tightened a cinch on the third animal. "You take that roan, ma'am," he said, indicating a large, leggy stallion. "Here's your regular horse, Bronco," he continued, handing the reins of a small chestnut pony to the young rider. "And this 'un is yours," Hobson said to George.

George looked at the animal. The animal looked at George. Both snorted and frowned. The animal stomped its hoof and kicked up dust. So did George.

"Why are my horse's ears so much longer than the others'?" George asked Mr. Hobson suspiciously.

"He's a good listener," Hobson said, helping George to mount the short, stubby beast.

"Don't I have another choice, Mr. Hobson?" George asked, after noticing that his boots nearly reached the ground.

"Yup. You got Hobson's choice," replied Hobson. "You ride Sea Biscuit here, or you walk."

"I'll take Sea Biscuit," George said, reaching for the reins.

"Let's hit the trail," Kate said. She dug in her heels, and the big roan hit the trail at a run. Bronco followed. George dug in his heels, too, but nothing much seemed to happen.

Bronco and Kate rode away at a gallop while George, atop Sea Biscuit, strolled after them through the cloud of dust.

"Giddy-up," said George.

"Hee-haw," said Sea Biscuit.

* * *

Dusk was falling as Bronco reined in his mount on the edge of a high desert mesa. Long shadows stretched across the red-tinted sands. Kate pulled her horse up alongside the pony.

"Mulch Gulch," Bronco said, pointing at the valley that lay below. He squinted through the gathering murk. "Let's ride," he said.

"Wait," Kate said, laying a restraining hand on his arm. "We don't want to lose George."

They looked behind them along the trail. A small speck was barely visible zigzagging across the sand. Kate could just make out her partner's big white hat. She sighed.

wooden signs, creaking in the wind, dangled from rusty chains. Their faded paint announced a dry goods store, a saloon, a sheriff's office and jail, a blacksmith shop, a hotel, a courthouse, and even a long-defunct savings and loan. But no business had been done in any of the buildings for many a long year. Tattered cobwebs hung in the doorways. Dusty grit blew across gaping holes in the old wooden sidewalks.

"Hard to believe this was once a roaring mining town," Kate said as a tumbleweed rolled by.

"When the gold ran out, so did all the people." Bronco was used to the dreary scene. He was eager for them to move on. "The gold is buried just outside of town," he said, moving toward his pony. "Let's get a move on!"

"Whoa, Bronco," Kate said, holding up a hand. "It's late. That gold has been hidden for 150 years," she reminded her young friend. "Another 12 hours won't make any difference."

"She's right, Bronco," said George. "It's getting dark." He looked nervously around the shadowy ghost town. For a moment, George thought he heard voices in the wind. He shivered.

"I guess you're right," said Bronco. He wasn't hearing voices, but he was noticing storm clouds rolling in across the darkening sky.

"I say we make camp, rustle up some grub, and grab some shut-eye," George suggested.

"I don't know, George," Kate said, frowning. "I think we should find a place to pitch our tents, have dinner, and then go to sleep."

"That's what I . . . " George began. He stopped when he saw his partner's smile.

She aimed a finger at him and said "Gotcha."

* * *

Kate took one look at the filthy floorboards in Mulch Gulch's deserted buildings and declared them off limits for camping. "Even the ground's better than that," she announced.

They moseyed over to a flat spot on the outskirts of town, near a grove of scrub oak. When supper was over, Kate and Bronco started laying out their bedrolls. In the distance, lightning flashed and thunder rumbled.

"I brought some shelter-halves," George said, pointing to a pile of canvas near the fire. "You can use them if it rains."

"What about you, Mr. Frankly?" Bronco said, crawling into his bedroll.

"I'll be all right," George said bravely. He pulled some things from his saddlebag. "Don't worry about me." In moments he was fluffing up a down sleeping bag and placing it on a self-inflating air mattress. Then he rigged up a small, sleek one-man tent.

Kate had propped herself up on one elbow to watch her partner. "That's a nice setup, George," she said, raising an eyebrow. "I wish *I* had one."

"I bet you do," George said. While Kate and Bronco struggled to get comfortable, George whipped out a plump camping pillow and added it to his bedroll. "There. All done!"

But it wasn't until George pulled a guitar from a case that Kate sat up in surprise. "That's funny, George," she said, giving her partner a strange look. "I didn't notice a guitar case strapped to your mount."

"I'll say one thing for Sea Biscuit," George replied. "He sure makes a good packhorse."

George strummed the guitar and cleared his throat. "Any cowboy song requests?" he asked.

"Can you sing far, far away?" Bronco joked.

"I don't think I know that one," George said. "How about 'Blood on the Saddle'?"

"How about you go beddy-bye," Kate said. She yawned hugely. "I'm plumb tuckered out."

"Okay, okay," George said, somewhat miffed. He put the guitar away, pulled his boots off, and slipped into his bed-away-from-home. "Good night."

The three *caballeros* had just closed their eyes when a loud bang echoed through their camp. It wasn't thunder. It sounded again.

"Take cover!" George ordered in a loud voice. He scrambled out of his tent and pulled Bronco down behind a log. Kate quickly joined them. Another loud bang cracked the air, followed by a volley of gunshots.

"What's that?" Bronco asked, lifting his head for a look.

"Gunshots," Kate answered, pushing Bronco's head safely back behind the log.

"Gun *play*," George corrected. "Cowboys call it gun *play*, Kate."

As suddenly as they had begun, the gunshots stopped. The threesome looked at each other. One by one, their heads popped up from behind the log. No bullets came their way. Instead, new sounds could be heard.

"I hear laughing," said Bronco in a puzzled voice.

"And a piano," Kate observed. She looked at George. "You didn't pack a piano in those saddlebags, did you?" she asked.

George shook his head. More laughter and distant voices drifted toward them on the wind.

"Seems to be coming from town," George said nervously.

"It may be a ghost town," Kate said thoughtfully, "but it sounds like those ghosts know how to have a good time." She stood up and walked over to her boots. "Let's check it out, pardners."

George fumbled putting on his own boots. The spurs jangled faintly under his shaky hands. Gunshots had been bad enough, but *ghosts* . . . !

Stealthily the threesome approached the town on foot. The storm was almost upon them, and they squinted against the grit blowing in their eyes. As they reached the main street, they were amazed to see Mulch Gulch aglow. Lights blazed, and figures moved across the ragged curtains of its buildings. Snatches of conversation could be heard above the wind.

"Don't try anything foolish, Jaspar," boomed a deep voice.

"Why, you low-down polecat!" someone else snarled.

Another man threatened, "I oughta marry your face to that wall."

"You and whose army?" was the reply.

George looked around wildly. The street was empty.

"Reach for the skies, you four-flusher."

"I'm gonna drill ya!"

Kate met George's eyes and shook her head. She couldn't tell where the voices were coming from, either. The wind made everything sound strange.

George motioned for Kate to move ahead. The two kept low, heading for the saloon. They moved swiftly, their backs to the wooden walls.

The sounds continued. An occasional gunshot was heard, the piano music continued to play, and the laughter rose as the posse of do-gooders approached the saloon on tiptoe. The shadows of cowboys and dance hall girls flitted across the windows. Kate moved into position by the swinging doors.

"Don't let them see you," George whispered. Bronco nodded. He waited until Kate was safely out of sight and scooted after her.

Through deft maneuvering, George and Kate flanked the swinging doors, with Bronco shadowing Kate. George slipped the calculator from his holster, spun it, and nodded at the others solemnly. Kate rolled her eyes but returned the nod.

On George's signal, the nouveau-cowpokes burst into the saloon. As they charged through the doors, the room was plunged into silence and darkness.

DUM DE DUM DUM

CHAPTER
4

"Who turned out the lights?" Bronco's voice asked in the darkness.

"I don't know. I just got here," George's voice replied.

They were still for a moment. Not a sound could be heard save the overactive thumping of three cow-poke-hearts.

"Maybe they heard us and hightailed it out of here," Kate speculated.

"They didn't have to take the lights with them," George said.

The three of them stumbled around in the pitch-black saloon.

"It's so dark I can't see my hand in front of my face," Bronco complained.

"That's because it's *my* face," George said in a nasal voice, rubbing his nose.

"Sorry."

"Anybody got a match or a flashlight or *some-thing*?" Kate asked, exasperated.

"Yes," said George. "All three. But they're in my saddlebag."

"Well, we'll have to check it out tomorrow," Kate said. "We certainly can't do anything here tonight, so let's lowtail it back to camp."

"I'll tell you one thing," George said, as they headed out the doors.

"What?" Bronco wanted to know.

"This is the liveliest ghost town I ever saw."

* * *

On their return to camp, the cowpokes noted, with some concern, that all was not right with the world.

"George," Kate said, "didn't you just throw new logs on the fire before we turned in?"

"Yes, why?" he said.

"Because the fire is almost out." Kate pointed at the smoldering fire. "Someone appears to have kicked sand on it."

The three split up to scour the campsite for more signs of foul play.

"Mr. Frankly, Ms. Monday," yelled Bronco. He was playing his flashlight over the area. "Our horses are gone."

"What?" George said, incredulously.

"And look at this, Three Bears," Kate said. She poked her sleeping bag with the tip of her boot. "Someone has been sleeping in our bedrolls."

She was right. Someone had turned her bag inside out. Bronco's was in the same condition. George peeked in his tent. His inflatable mattress was flat as a pancake. So was his pillow.

"I'm glad there are no such things as ghosts," Bronco said, with a slight shiver, "because if there *were*, I would bet they've been here."

As he spoke, rain began to fall heavily.

"It figures," George said, looking to the heavens. "When it rains, it pours."

* * *

The next morning dawned crisp and clear. Kate opened her eyes to see her partner cooking bacon and eggs over an open fire. The aroma of fresh coffee was carried to her by a slight breeze. Her nose twitched.

"Morning, Pard." George grinned. He poured some coffee and handed her a mug. "Have a cup of mud."

Kate crawled out of her bedroll. She peered down at the fire. "Where'd you get the fresh eggs?" she asked curiously.

"I brought a chicken from home," George answered.

Kate stared at George suspiciously. Then she shrugged and held out her plate.

Bronco appeared a moment later. He had been scouting the stand of scrub oaks. "Morning, Ms. Monday," he said glumly. "I've been looking for the horses, but the rain washed all their tracks away."

"We'll look for them later," George said. "Let's

chow down and head for town."

Fortified by scrambled eggs, home fries, and OJ, Bronco was soon in a better mood and raring to investigate the ghost town. George was less raring, but he figured that ghosts wouldn't make an appearance in daylight, so he led the march into Mulch Gulch.

Moments later they were standing in a phalanx at the head of Front Street. Their shadows stretched ahead of them down the dusty thoroughfare. A tumbleweed tumbled by. George looked to his left at Bronco and to his right at Kate and nodded. The threesome moved forward in a row, watching out of the corners of their eyes for any false moves. The only sound was the *chink* of George's spurs.

Chink chink.

Chink chink.

BANG!

The sound of a single gunshot cracked the still air, and George Frankly fell to earth.

"I'm hit," he cried out in a voice filled with pain. "I'm hit."

Kate and Bronco knelt beside their fallen comrade. As Bronco tried to gently roll George over onto his back, Kate kept a close lookout for the gunman. There was no one in sight.

"It's getting dark, Kate." George grimaced.

"George . . . " Kate had been examining her partner.

"Tell Martha my insurance policies are in my sock drawer under the argyles." George coughed weakly.

"George . . . " Kate said again. There were no

bloodstains that she could see. "Please, Kate," George said. His voice was fading. "I'm a-goin'."

That's when Kate noticed a heavy cord wrapped around her fallen friend's boot heel.

"George!" Kate said, pulling at the cord. "You're not shot. You just tripped over this."

George sat up. He looked down at himself in surprise.

"No bullet holes," he said happily. "What a relief. I thought I was a goner."

Kate got to her feet. George and Bronco watched as she tugged at the cord. It rose up from the dusty street, where it had been concealed in the dirt.

"George." Kate pulled at the electrical cord. More of it emerged from the dirt. "Doesn't something strike you as a bit unusual?"

"Yes," George said, struggling to his feet. "High-heeled boots aren't as easy to walk in as I thought." He dusted himself off and rubbed a sore knee.

"An electrical cord," said Bronco, catching on quicker than his new friend. "What's an electrical cord doing in a town that never had electricity?"

"Exactly," said Kate. She slowly unearthed the cord and followed it toward the saloon. George and Bronco followed. Together they peered past the honky-tonk's swinging doors.

Sitting at one of the saloon's rickety tables was a wizened old man. He was bent over the table, working on a battered tape recorder. Kate looked down at the cord in her hands. It was attached to the recorder.

Kate gave a strong yank on the wire. Inside the

saloon the recorder flew off the table and crashed onto the floor. The old man turned, amazed and frightened. He spotted the threesome in the doorway.

"You shot it right outa my hands," he said to Kate, looking at the smashed recorder.

"Put 'em up," George said, shouldering through the doors. The bearded man looked at the calculator pointed at him and thrust his hands toward the sky.

"Who are you?" the prisoner asked in admiration.

"Mathematicians," George answered shortly. He kept his calculator trained on the old man.

"Who are *you*?" Kate asked.

"Name's Rommel," Rommel said, nervously.

"Rommel the desert fox?" George squinted at the old man. He didn't *look* like a famous dead wartime general.

"No." Rommel shook his head, still with his hands in the air. "That was my cousin. I'm Rommel the desert *rat*. Scruffy Rommel."

Kate's eyebrows rose. So this was the man Mutard had warned them about.

George continued the questioning. "You weren't playing tape recordings of gunshots and saloon fights and dance hall music last night, were you?" he asked.

"Sure was," said Rommel, smiling proudly, underneath a wild and woolly dingy white beard. His smile revealed that he had a few teeth missing.

"Were you trying to scare us away?" Bronco asked Scruffy.

"That was the general i-dee." Scruffy's arms started to droop, but he hurriedly straightened them.

"Trying to stop us from coming back?" Kate guessed.

Scruffy nodded. "That 'bout covers it."

"It almost worked," George admitted. "Where'd you hide the generator?"

"Behind a tree," Scruffy said, gesturing with his hand.

"Did you wreck our camp and steal our horses, too?" Bronco asked.

"Yep. The horses're down the street in the livery stable." Scruffy pointed with his elbow, since his arms were still in the air.

"Why did you do it, Scruffy?" Kate wondered.

"Because I want to be alone," said the old man. "Got no use fer people. They ruined civilization." He sighed. "That's how come I moved to a ghost town. So's I could just sit back all by my lonesome and do nothin'."

"What did you used to do?" George asked.

Scruffy wrinkled his nose. "Not much. A long ways back I was an account exec with an advertising agency in the East. Pretty successful, too. But one day I just up and quit."

George nodded wisely. "Couldn't stand the pressure?" he guessed.

Scruffy shook his head. "Nope. Couldn't stand the commute. Ever travel between Greenwich, Connecticut, and New York City twice a day on a mule?"

Bronco watched Scruffy as he laughed, but he had something more important on his mind. "Shouldn't we get our horses and start looking for . . . you-know-what?" he said impatiently to George and Kate.

Scruffy gave Bronco one of his gap-toothed grins. "Here to look for Capone's gold, I s'pose," he said, cackling.

"How did you know?" Bronco gasped.

"It's the only reason anybody ever comes here." Scruffy shrugged as best he could in his position. "If you want my opinion, I don't think there ever was any such gold. Just one of them tall tales."

Bronco just smiled and shook his head. Scruffy didn't know about the map.

"Well, we've solved one mystery," Kate said, heading for the door. "Now, let's go for the gold."

"Mind if I tag along?" Scruffy asked.

"Why not?" Kate smiled.

The desert rat looked up at his hands, cleared his throat loudly and added, "Mind if I put my arms down now?"

* * *

Rommel led everyone to the rundown stables, where the treasure-seekers found their mounts contentedly chomping on some hay. Bronco said he knew the general area where their search should start. Together the foursome rode to the edge of town. When Bronco gave the signal, they dismounted and tethered their horses to some nearby scrub.

Bronco oriented the map and began pointing out the landmarks.

"See," he said, patting a large rock, "here's the rock. And over there is the oak tree. It's got to be that really tall, thick one," Bronco reasoned, "because it's the only one old enough to have been around 150 years ago.

"Good cogitating, Bronco," Kate said. She had been doing some thinking herself. She began to pace the distance between the rock and the oak tree.

Rommel was watching Kate in bewilderment. "Funny time to take a stroll," he said, leaning against the rock.

George explained his partner's actions. "If our map is to scale, Scruffy, that will help us determine where to dig."

"Ten paces," Kate announced. "That's about 10 yards, or 30 feet."

Bronco smoothed out the map on the rock. They all crowded close for a look.

George whipped out a ruler and placed it on the map.

Kate pointed. "On the map, the rock is 6 inches from the tree."

"We know that in reality that's a distance of 30 feet," George said. "That means 1 inch stands for 5 feet."

Scruffy was unimpressed. "Yeah? So where's the gold?" he demanded.

"One step at a time," Kate scolded. "To find the exact spot we'll have to use a trigonometric operation called triangulation. It's part of mathematics."

"Look at the map," George said. "We first draw a line between the rock and the tree. Then another line between the tree and the arrow, and another between the rock and the arrow."

Reflection of map says to "Dig Heer"

"Hey, you made one of them three-sided what-chamacallits," Scruffy said, scratching his beard with both hands.

"A triangle," George said. "Now, if we had a protractor . . . "

Scruffy was flummoxed again. "A what?"

"A protractor is an instrument used to measure angles," George supplied.

"I thought a *pro*-tractor was a tractor that played for money," Scruffy said.

Kate and George stared at the old man. Then they shook their heads and turned back to the map.

"If we had a protractor, we could measure the angles on the map, then lay them out on the ground," George said. "Each of us then could walk in a straight line—" he traced his fingers on the map—"and where we meet would be about where we should dig," he concluded.

"But we ain't got no protractor," Scruffy said. "So we're sunk."

"Not necessarily," Kate interjected. "If the map is to scale, and 1 inch stands for 5 feet . . . "

She measured the distance between the rock and the arrow.

"Eight inches. And between the tree and the arrow . . . 10 inches," Kate muttered. "Forty and 50 feet. We need a rope," she said, looking around.

Bronco ran to the horses and retrieved two lariats.

"We don't know how long these are," Kate said. She looked her partner up and down. "How tall are you, George?"

" I'm 6 feet, 1/8 inch," George said, standing up a bit straighter.

Kate held one end of the rope at the top of George's head and dropped the rest. Then she bent and picked up the rope at the point right above the heel of his boot.

Scruffy applauded. "Hey," he said, "now you got 6 feet of rope. That is, if your friend there is to scale."

Kate doubled the rope length for 12 feet, then again and once again for 48 feet. She estimated 2 feet and tied a knot in the lariat. "That's about 50 feet," she said.

George was doing the same with the second length of rope. He counted out 40 feet and made a knot.

"Forty feet from the rock to the arrow," Bronco reminded them. "Fifty feet from the tree to the arrow."

George took the 50-foot length of rope and held one end against the tree. Bronco took the 40-foot length to the rock, while Scruffy and Kate played down the ropes to their respective knots.

At Kate's signal, she and Scruffy walked toward one another until they met. "This must be the spot marked by the arrow," Kate said. She scraped an X in the dirt. "X marks the spot," she announced.

* * *

Holes in hardpan are not easy to make, not even with the shovels and picks George had brought along. An hour later, the hole was only 3 feet deep.

"Your turn," said Kate wearily, climbing out of the

hole and handing her shovel to George.

"Boy, there's never a backhoe around when you need one," George said, wiping his brow. He dug for a few minutes in silence.

"I keep thinking my next shovelful will go *clunk* on a treasure chest," George huffed. He thrust his shovel into the heavy clay and heard a *clunk*.

"Do you think that's it?" Kate asked excitedly.

Scruffy and Bronco began digging like madmen. Within a minute they unearthed a small strongbox.

"We found it," Bronco shouted, dragging the chest from the hole. "The gold must be inside."

George lifted a pick with a dramatic flourish. He placed the steel tip through the shackle of the rusted padlock and twisted it. The lock snapped apart. Slowly, George lifted the lid. The old lid creaked loudly as it showed its contents to the sunlight for the first time in 150 years. Kate, George, Scruffy, and Bronco all held their breaths as they stared into the musty box.

DUM DE DUM DUM

CHAPTER
5

"There's nothing in it!" Bronco wailed.

"Yes, there is," George assured him, as he reached inside and removed a single scrap of paper. It was covered with squiggles and a scribbled message.

"'Uthr prt uv map C. Myrer 1853,'" George read, with a sinking heart.

"What?" cried Bronco. He couldn't believe that after all his hard work, the treasure was just a piece of paper with scribbling on it.

"Let's head back to camp," said Kate. "We can sit down and think about how to solve this puzzle."

An hour later, the forlorn foursome sat around the campsite pondering the aged note. Scruffy played a mournful tune on his harmonica.

"Other part of map, C. Myrer 1853," George said for the dozenth time.

"What could it mean?" Bronco asked. The discovery of the note had left him still somewhat despondent.

"Well," Kate mused, "it could mean that in 1853 someone named Charlie Myrer had another part of the map."

"Who's Charlie Myrer?" Scruffy asked, taking the harmonica from his lips.

Kate shrugged. "Or Claudia or Calvin . . . somebody whose first name starts with C."

"Whoever C. Myrer was, he or she is history by now," Bronco said glumly. Then his face brightened. "You know, if we could find out who this person was, maybe we could still find the other part of the map."

"How?" asked Scruffy, scratching his stomach.

"Well, it could be in a house Myrer owned around here," George suggested.

"We've got those books Bronco borrowed from Mr. Mutard's library," Kate reminded them. "Maybe one of them has a census in it."

"What's a census?" Bronco asked, frowning.

"It's a list of people who live around here at a particular time," George explained.

Kate said, "You check that, George." She turned to Scruffy. "Are any records still stored in these old buildings?" she asked. The old man nodded. "Then I'll go to the Mulch Gulch Courthouse and check the register of deeds," Kate said.

She smiled at Bronco, who was waiting eagerly for his assignment. "Bronco, why don't you and Scruffy check Boot Hill," she suggested, mentioning the cemetery she'd noticed by the town. "See if somebody named C. Myrer is buried there." Kate looked around at the others' bright faces. "They're long shots, but at least they're shots."

For the next few hours, the cowpokes worked feverishly at their jobs. Kate went through moldy tomes of records left behind in the ghost town's courthouse. She was unable to come up with any land owned by a C. Myrer.

"Maybe ol' C. Myrer was just passing through," she reasoned to herself, "And a visit from a stranger might have been written up in the local press." She headed for the newspaper office to check back issues covered in decades of dust.

Meanwhile, George poured over the nineteenth-century history books on the area.

Outside town, Scruffy and Bronco wandered through the cemetery searching for the name C. Myrer.

"It sure is dead up here," Scruffy said. He pulled out his harmonica and played a blues in C minor.

Bronco dodged in and around looking at every tombstone. He found no C. Myrer. He sighed, "Let's go see if the others had any luck. There's *nothing* here."

They found the others in the newspaper office. Each admitted that, so far, their searches were futile.

"No census in any of those books?" Kate asked.

George shook his head. "It's probably in the Kern County Library," he said. "But that's too far to travel today."

"On the way here I noticed a pay phone. It's only a few miles back," Kate said, by way of suggestion.

"Oh, Kate . . . " George whined, rubbing his back.

"I'd go, Pard," Kate said. She pointed to the old newspapers. "But I have to finish my task."

George sighed, went outside, and saddled Sea Biscuit. Sea Biscuit was not particularly happy to see George.

"Giddy-up," George instructed. "How about a gallop?"

The donkey gave a less than enthusiastic "Heehaw" and strolled off down the road.

* * *

Many long saddle-sore miles later, George was standing in a phone booth. He was arguing with the telephone operator.

"But operator, I don't have any change," George said, emptying the pockets of his chaps.

"Then you can't talk on my telephone," said the tinny voice on the other end of the line.

"But it's very important," George pleaded.

"I'll just bet a cookie it is," the operator sneered. "But you can't talk without change."

"Will you take a check?" George stared at the buzzing phone. The operator had hung up.

"Got a quarter?" George asked Sea Biscuit.

By the time George had convinced the operator to put his call through he was not in a good mood. It didn't make him any happier when he reached D. John Mutard and the librarian's first word was "Shhhhh!"

George identified himself and asked if the library had census figures for the years 1851 through 1860.

"Most certainly," Mr. Mutard said.

George asked him to check those years for the name C. Myrer and waited while the librarian searched his records.

"Sorry, Mr. Frankly," he said, "but no one by that name lived in Mulch Gulch at that time."

"Rats," George muttered. "I thought we had the gold for sure this time. See, we found this note with a clue to the gold. It's got something to do with this C. Myrer."

"Never heard of the individual," Mutard muttered back.

George cheered up. "Well, Kate's probably tracked him down. Thanks anyway, Mr. Mutard."

"My pleasure to serve," the librarian said. "My pleasure, indeed."

DUM DE DUM DUM

CHAPTER
6

The next day found George, Kate, and Bronco in the Mulch Gulch saloon, drinking sarsaparillas and looking at the C. Myrer note.

"Don't you want to sit down, George?" Kate asked, leaning back in her chair.

"No, thanks," George said, "Sea Biscuit took a lot of the fun out of sitting yesterday." He leaned against the wall.

Bronco looked at the paper and moaned, "We're all right back where we started."

Kate looked around the saloon. "No, we aren't. One of us is missing. Where's Scruffy?"

George and Bronco both shrugged.

"I haven't see him this morning," Bronco said. "Now that I think about it, he left kind of suddenly after dinner last night."

"I guess he got tired of so many people," Kate said. "After all, he came here to get away from civilization."

George frowned. He was wondering if there was a more sinister reason for Scruffy's disappearance. Maybe the old man had discovered a clue, or had even found the gold, or . . .

George's grim thoughts were interrupted by Kate.

"Maybe it's time to play What-If," she suggested.

"What's that?" asked Bronco.

"A little game we Mathnetters play to try to get our facts in order," Kate answered. "It can help you lay out a problem. Like this . . . "

She thought for a moment. "What if . . . this C. Myrer was Capone's partner and lived in another town?"

"Then there'd be no record of him in Mulch Gulch," George replied.

"What if . . . C. Myrer was Capone's wife and Myrer was her maiden name?" was Kate's next guess.

George shook his head. "Why would Mrs. Capone use her maiden name?"

"Maybe she used it professionally," Kate said in a doubtful voice.

Bronco joined the game. "What if C. Myrer isn't a person?"

Kate and George stared at Bronco in admiration.

"What if . . . the word means something else?" the boy continued.

George thought, "*My*-rer doesn't mean anything. Neither does My-*rer*."

"How about mir-ror?" Bronco said. He started jumping up and down in his chair. The worn-out seat creaked in protest. "How about 'See mirror'?"

"That's not how Capone spelled it," George said.

"But we know Capone was a bad speller," Kate said, getting excited, too. "'See mirror'! That's got to be it. Other part of map see mirror."

Kate looked at the long mirror behind the bar. Its heavy gilded frame was encrusted in dust. Suddenly she rushed around the bar. The others followed with the map in hand.

"The reflection!" Bronco shouted. "We used the reflection of the first map to find the first clue. Maybe we should do the same with this note."

"But this mirror isn't curved like the thermos," Kate pointed out.

"But we can still use the reflection," said Bronco. "Remember that ambulance we saw in the rearview mirror in the car?"

Kate nodded. She held the message, with its odd squiggles and lines, up to the mirror.

"Nothing," Kate said.

"Turn it around," Bronco said.

Kate rotated the paper 90 degrees. Still nothing.

"Wait," George said. "Hold the *edge* of the map up to the mirror."

Kate did as he suggested. Suddenly, among one group of lines, the letters HEX were revealed in the mirror.

George smiled. "See. Look at those letters . . .

they're symmetrical. If you put a mirror along one half,"—he placed the map to the mirror—"you see the other half."

Bronco shrugged. "Yeah, I see. But did Capone do that on purpose? I don't think he was that smart. After all, he misspelled all those words . . . ."

"That's it!" Kate cried.

"Bronco, you've done it again," George said approvingly.

"What?" Bronco was pleased, but he didn't know why. "What'd I do?"

"Capone misspelled his message," George explained. He pointed to the map.

"Get it?" George said triumphantly. "*Hex* marks the spot!" He pointed, "We should dig there."

Bronco frowned. "Dig where? *Where* is the spot? There aren't any landmarks on this map."

Kate snapped her fingers and said, "Maybe there aren't *two* separate maps. Maybe there's just one!"

Bronco's eyes lit up. He pulled out the first map and spread it out on the bar. Kate laid the second sheet beside it. She slid them together.

They match," George said, clapping Kate on the back. "This is the 'uthr prt uv map'! Let's ride, pardners."

* * *

The mathematicians knew that the first half of the map was to scale. They decided to work on the assumption that the second was as well. Using triangulation once again, George and Bronco used their lengths of rope to locate the spot marked HEX.

George scraped an X in the dirt as Kate arrived with shovels and picks.

"I'm sorry Scruffy isn't here to see this," Bronco said as he lunged at the dirt with his shovel.

"I'm sorry he isn't here to help dig," said George, who was still feeling suspicious of the missing desert rat.

They dug and dug. The hole was pretty deep and they were about to give up when they heard the telltale sound.

Clunk.

"Hear that? It was a *clunk*!" George said excitedly.

They dropped to their knees and brushed away the dirt. A second strongbox was revealed.

George and Kate forced the rusted lock open. They lifted the lid.

"Yi!!" Bronco let out a loud whoop. There, before them, were hundreds of gold nuggets.

"The gold," said Kate.

"And it's all yours," George said to Bronco. "You deserve it, after all your work. What are you going to do with it?"

"He's going to give it to me," said a voice from above them, no louder than a whisper. "And he's going to do it *now*."

They looked up to see a pale figure dressed in black standing at the edge of the hole. He was pointing a large Colt revolver at them.

"D. John Mutard," George exclaimed.

"Shhhhh. Not so loud," Mutard shushed, pointing the gun directly at the Mathnetter.

"I should have known he wasn't a true librarian," George said in disgust. "They never really say 'Shhhhh.'"

"What do you think you're doing, Mutard?" Kate demanded.

"I've come to claim what is mine. Put your hands in the air," the librarian whispered.

"Yours? *We* found the gold," Bronco protested. "Not you."

"Saddlesore Capone was my great-grandfather on my mother's side," Mutard retorted. "That gold belongs to me."

"But Capone stole the gold," Kate said reasonably. "It wasn't his to begin with."

"Don't be a nit-picker, and stop your whining,"

Mutard snapped in a sinister whisper glaring down at them.

"Mutard," George said, "you're giving librarians the world over a very bad name."

Mutard merely sneered.

Suddenly a voice boomed, from beyond the hole's edge, "Reach for the skies, you four-flusher."

"Don't try anything foolish, Jaspar," snarled a second.

"You low-down polecat, I'm agonna drill you," came the third.

More voices filled the air with dire threats. D. John Mutard dropped his gun and thrust his arms skyward. He trembled as gunshots rang through the air.

But George, Kate and Bronco had recognized the voices—and the gunshots. They clambered out of the hole in time to see Scruffy swing off his horse. The desert rat turned a portable tape recorder off and collected Mutard's gun.

"Scruffy," George said, pumping the old man's arm, "you are a sight for sore eyes." George was sorry he'd ever suspected the old man. "But why'd you leave?" He had to know.

"I needed some peace and quiet to do some thinkin'. I'm not used to so many people being around," Scruffy said. "And I started wonderin' . . . what if C. Myrer wasn't a name after all but some sort of instruction . . . something like 'See mirror.' Make any sense?"

George nodded, grinning. Then he finished tying Mutard's hands together.

"It makes perfect sense, Scruffy." Kate pecked a kiss on the small part of the old man's face not covered with hair. "Absolutely perfect sense."

DUM DE DUM DUM

EPILOGUE

D. John Mutard was convicted of a 211, attempted robbery, and a 020.313, disgracing the Dewey Decimal System. Bronco Guillermo Gomez took the $90,000 and invested it for his college education, hoping that by the time he was ready, it would be enough to cover his freshman year.

ACTIVITIES

MEASURING, BY GEORGE

Kate, George, and Bronco had to measure off 40 and 50 feet to find the treasure. But they didn't have a measuring tape. Luckily, Kate decided to use George as a ruler because he's about six feet. Then she estimated two feet.

Using +6, -6, +2, -2 and 2x, can you come up with at least two ways to get to 40? (Remember, they can also subtract 6 feet or 2 feet of rope at any time.)

TOO MANY SALOONS

When they got to Mulch Gulch, Kate and George had to match their scrap of a map to landmarks in the ghost town.

Here is a map of Main Street in Mulch Gulch today.

Since 1853, things have changed. The Mathnet team knows that a treasure is hidden under the floorboards of an old saloon, which was exactly the same distance from the bank as it was from the livery stable.

The problem is there are now four saloons in Mulch Gulch. The bank was closed and a hotel built in its place! By counting the measures, can you figure out which saloon they should look in?

Suppose the bank had been only half as far from the saloon as the livery stable. Which saloon would the treasure be in?

MIRROR, MIRROR

Bronco, Kate, and George use a mirror to discover that letters H, E, and X are horizontally symmetrical. That means the top half is a mirror image of the bottom half.

Some letters like A, T, and O are *vertically symmetrical*. Can you figure out what that means?

When the Mathnetters returned to base, George decided to play a trick on Kate and hide her badge. He tells her that symmetry can help her find it, and writes these figures on the board.

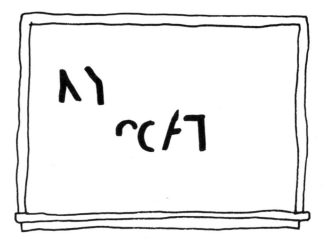

He gives her a small mirror. Can you find out where George has hidden Kate's badge?

After figuring out where her badge is, Kate leaves George a symmetry puzzle on the board and gives him the mirror. What does Kate tell George?

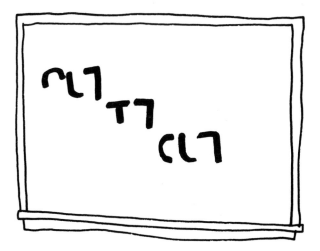

ANSWERS

MEASURING BY GEORGE

Here are two ways to get 40 feet using the six and two foot lengths of rope:

$6 + 6 + 6 = 18$
$+ 2 = 20$
$x \ 2 = 40$

$6 \times 2 = 12$
$x \ 2 = 24$
$x \ 2 = 48$
$- 6 = 42$
$- 2 = 40$

You may have found another way.

TOO MANY SALOONS

The bank and the livery stable were the same distance from the saloon, so the treasure is in saloon number 3.

If the bank had been only half as far from the saloon as the livery stable then the treasure would be in saloon number 2.

MIRROR, MIRROR

#1 MY COAT

#2 CUT IT OUT

By the way, the letters of the alphabet that are horizontally symmetrical are: B, C, D, E, H, I, K, O, X

The ones that have a vertical line of symmetry are:
A, H, I, M, O, T, U, V, W, X, Y